Unknown Facts

Unknown Facts

Everything you wanted to know that you

don't know because it's unknown

by The Unknown Comic

Printed in the United States of America

Initial Printing, 2019

ISBN: 9781792857294

Unknown Publishing
Burbank, CA 91510

www.realunknowncomic.com

The Unknown Comic first tried using a plastic bag over his head but kept blacking out after the first joke.

The Unknown Comic once tried using a vacuum cleaner bag over his head... but that sucked.

After telling a joke about the mafia, they tried putting a cement bag over the Unknown Comic's head.

The Unknown Comic has been in the "Sack" with more women than any other celebrity.

The Unknown Comics favorite song is, "He ain't Hefty, he's my baggie."

Two Muslims once tried to pick up the Unknown Comic with the bag over his head, thinking he was a chick.

The Unknown Comic's wife's nickname is douche bag.

Chapter One

Random Unknown Facts

Unknown Fact:

Unicorns are real but they're fat and grey and are called Rhinos.

Unknown Fact:

Jewish mothers believe a fetus stays a fetus until it graduates from Medical School.

❖

Unknown Fact:

"Etc."... is used to make people think we know a lot more than we do.

❑

—

Unknown Fact:

Laughing is the best medicine unless you're laughing for no reason. Then you need medicine.

○

Unknown Fact:

The sun travels at 186,000 miles per second, but it's all downhill.

〰

Unknown Fact:

Alcohol is not the answer, but it does make you forget the question.

♦

Unknown Fact:

Removing the windshield wipers from your car will cut down on getting parking tickets.

❏

Unknown Fact:

The best way to keep from crying while cutting up onions is to not get emotionally attached.

Unknown Fact:

"Patience"... is what parents have when there are lots of people around.

Unknown Fact:

Water is used more for making oceans than for anything else.

Unknown Fact:

Two halves make a hole and then the quarterback goes through.

❖

Unknown Fact:

Money can't buy happiness, but it keeps the kids in touch.

○

Unknown Fact:

Money can't buy love...but it can put you in a good bargaining position.

〰

Unknown Fact:

It's impossible for a guy to look macho on the back of a motorcycle holding onto another guy.

◆

Unknown Fact:

Boomerangs are Frisbees for people who have no friends.

Unknown Fact:

The reason so many people are not working is because they're unemployed.

◆

Unknown Fact:

A wild goose is one that is more than an inch off center.

Unknown Fact:

What doesn't kill you makes you stronger... except for an angry gorilla. An angry gorilla will kill you.

Unknown Fact:

The speed of lightning would be faster if it didn't zig zag.

□

Unknown Fact:

The problem with being a good listener is that too many people want to talk to you.

Unknown Fact:

A verbal contract is not worth the paper it's written on.

Unknown Fact:

A lawyer is an expert on justice the same way a hooker is an expert on love.

Unknown Fact:

Teaching your dog to stand on one leg is a total waste of time.

◆

Unknown Fact:

Brigham Young was not a polygamist. He only had one wife, but she had 37 Wigs.

□

Unknown Fact:

Expecting the unexpected means that the unexpected is actually expected.

●

Unknown Fact:

Half of all politicians want to be discovered and the other half are afraid of being discovered.

∿

Unknown Fact:

Reality shows tend to take our minds off our minds.

❖

Unknown Fact:

The best way to embarrass a psychic is to throw them a surprise party.

❑

Unknown Fact:

An erection does not count as personal growth.

〰

Unknown Fact:

Googling your symptoms when you feel sick is the quickest way to convince yourself that you're dying.

○

Unknown Fact:

The three best things in life are a glass of wine before and a nap after.

◻

Unknown Fact:

Too many people buy life insurance then die anyway.

■

Unknown Fact:

A penny saved is not very much.

❐

Unknown Fact:

Redneck murders are hard to solve because there are no dental records and all the DNA is the same.

❐

Unknown Fact:

The world really isn't worse off. There's just better news coverage.

☒

Unknown Fact:

It was the Irish who invented the bagpipes who then gave it to the Scots, telling them it was a musical instrument.

Unknown Fact:

No matter how hard you try, you cannot baptize a cat.

Unknown Fact:

Time may be a great healer but it's a lousy beautician.

Unknown Fact:

On the Canary Islands there is not one canary. Same thing with the Virgin Islands. There is also not one canary there either.

Unknown Fact:

If you poop in holy water, it becomes holy shit.

~~~

Unknown Fact:

You can always find whatever you want when you don't want it by looking where it wouldn't be if you did want it.

●

Unknown Fact:

You cannot think outside the box when no one will come over and let you out of it.

❑

Unknown Fact:

Without your friends, you'd be a Total Stranger.

☒

Unknown Fact:

America has the best politicians money can buy.

□

Unknown Fact:

What goes up must come down... unless it orbits.

Unknown Fact:

Sinning is the best part of repentance.

❖

Unknown Fact:

Drinking gets rid of pimples. Not on you, but the one person you picked up at the bar.

▓

Unknown Fact:

The best way to start the day is to go back to bed.

◆

Unknown Fact:

A "Diamond" is one of the hardest substances known to man...especially, to get back.

Unknown Fact:

Trains are not afraid of cars.

●

Unknown Fact:

If a friend tells you, "Cheer up. Things could be worse." When you cheer up, things will get worse.

❑

Unknown Fact:

You can swim 100 yards in 3 seconds going over a waterfall.

~~~

Unknown Fact:

Instant messaging began with giving the finger.

♦

Unknown Fact:

A troublemaker rarely has trouble making trouble.

○

Unknown Fact:

Most people don't need to be led into temptation. They can easily find it on their own.

~~~

Unknown Fact:

Fat chance and slim chance mean the same thing.

☒

Unknown Fact:

Your body will not absorb the calories from food taken from another person's plate.

〰

Unknown Fact:

Learning to play a harp does not improve your chances of getting to heaven.

❑

Unknown Fact:

If you sit on your hand until it's numb, when you masturbate, it will feel like a total stranger.

●

Unknown Fact:

It's never a good idea to pet a raccoon when you're drunk.

Unknown Fact:

Nervous breakdowns show you care.

●

Unknown Fact:

You should never trust anyone who has stolen money from me more than five times.

♒

Unknown Fact:

"Pain" usually strikes the body at its weakest point which is why "Headaches" are so common.

■

—

Unknown Fact:

A mouse trap placed on your alarm clock will prevent you from rolling over and going back to sleep after you hit the snooze button.

Unknown Fact:

Pigeon shit is not good luck.

♦

Unknown Fact:

People who are worth twenty million dollars or more are better looking.

❑

Unknown Fact:

If you're playing poker and you look around the table and can't tell who the sucker is, it's you.

●

Unknown Fact:

If you keep all your money under your mattress, you'll always have something to fall back on.

~~~

Unknown Fact:

If God were a woman, most of us would go to Hell without even knowing why.

❑

Unknown Fact:

Adam and Eve were the first people to not read the Apple terms and conditions.

■

Unknown Fact:

Despite the cost of living being so high, it still remains popular.

Unknown Fact:

People who fly planes look down on people who don't.

●

Unknown Fact:

Money is just green stuff with pictures of dead people on it.

◆

Unknown Fact:

A chrysanthemum by any other name would be easier to spell.

❖

Unknown Fact:

Revenge is a dish best served naked.

〰

Unknown Fact:

If you want to find inner peace...take Tums.

○

Unknown Fact:

The human brain is an amazing organ which works 24 hours a day every second of everyday from the time you leave the womb until you find religion.

❏

Unknown Fact:

The best way to kill an hour in New York City is to drive around the block.

☒

Unknown Fact:

If one door closes and another door opens, you're probably in prison.

■

Unknown Fact:

If you can build a better mousetrap... you'll catch better mice.

◻

Unknown Fact:

If you change your car horn to gunshot sounds, people move out of the way much faster.

〰

Unknown Fact:

Einstein's favorite jokes were wisecracks.

⌂

Unknown Fact:

A great way to meet new people in a bar is to pick up someone else's change.

Unknown Fact:

The best way to keep your kitchen spotless and clean is to eat out.

Unknown Fact:

You can lead a Politician to congress... but you can't make them think.

Unknown Fact:

The only time a politician is telling the truth is when he's calling another politician a liar.

⊠

Unknown Fact:

All fairy tales do NOT begin with, "Once upon a time..." Some begin with, "Honey, I got stuck at the office..."

■

Unknown Fact:

"Velcro" is a rip off!

Unknown Fact:

The polar bear is the stupidest animal in the jungle.

Unknown Fact:

The mosquito was discovered by a man who was discovered by a mosquito.

Unknown Fact:

The first guy who discovered milk did a lot of other weird shit too.

⊠

Unknown Fact:

The need to pee intensifies one hundred times when you're trying to unlock your front door.

Unknown Fact:

If God didn't want us to play with ourselves, He wouldn't have made our hands reach that far.

Unknown Fact:

Intelligent people swear more than stupid motherfuckers.

Unknown Fact:

In Miami, you're not considered legally dead until you lose your tan.

Unknown Fact:

Money can't buy happiness, but it can buy wine and that's very close to happiness.

Unknown Fact:

It's considered rude to wear a tie to an orgy.

□

Unknown Fact:

If Mexico ever stops sending drugs across the border.... Americans will be climbing the wall.

◆

Unknown Fact:

Taking sleeping pills will make you drowsy.

□

Unknown Fact:

Everyone should learn a trade, so that they will always know what kind of work they're out of.

☒

Unknown Fact:

If you cross a hungry cat with a mouse, you'll no longer have a hungry cat.

○

Unknown Fact:

If life was fair...horses would be riding us half the time.

♒

Unknown Fact:

If you go outside and it's cold, it's cold outside.

◆

Unknown Fact:

If your palm itches, you're going to get something. If your groin itches, you've already got something.

❑

Unknown Fact:

"A Wise Man is still a Fool to an Idiot."

☒

Unknown Fact:

Under Communism, man exploits man...but under capitalism, it's exactly the opposite.

⌘

Unknown Fact:

Life is what you make it until someone comes along and makes it worse.

〰

Unknown Fact:

Never write on an empty stomach... use paper.

Unknown Fact:

If laughter really was the best medicine, doctors would have figured a way to charge us for it.

Unknown Fact:

It's not really drinking alone if the dog is home.

Unknown Fact:

Whales prefer swimming in salt water because pepper water makes them sneeze.

Unknown Fact:

An apple a day will keep anyone away - if you throw it hard enough.

Unknown Fact:

If you cheat on your diet, you will gain in the end.

Unknown Fact:

Crime doesn't pay but cops don't earn that much either.

Unknown Fact:

If pigs could fly...the price of bacon would skyrocket.

Unknown Fact:

The secret of youth is lying about your age.

⊠

Unknown Fact:

If voting could really change things, it would be illegal.

◻

Unknown Fact:

The key to happiness is staying away from assholes.

◯

Unknown Fact:

Your boss is late when you're early and always early when you're late.

◼

Unknown Fact:

If you want a stable relationship, get a horse.

Unknown Fact:

People who wear pajamas in public have either given up on life or are living life to the fullest.

≋

Unknown Fact:

It now costs more to go to a Hospital than it does to go to Medical School.

●

Unknown Fact:

5 minutes of extra sleep in the morning really does matter.

◸

Unknown Fact:

Anyone who sees a psychiatrist needs to have their head examined.

◆

Unknown Fact:

One of the most enjoyable sounds you can ever hear is that sound that people make when they stop talking.

Unknown Fact:

The only thing worse than people talking about you behind your back is people not talking about you behind your back.

❑

Unknown Fact:

The difference between politics and baseball is in baseball if you're caught stealing, you're out.

◻

Unknown Fact:

Teen-agers believe that cereal is an acceptable meal at any time of day or night.

Unknown Fact:

If you want to go to Vegas and return with a small fortune, go there with a large fortune.

Unknown Fact:

The discovery of the North Pole proved that there is no one sitting on top of the world.

Unknown Fact:

If you can't take a vacation to Europe, you can get the same effect by staying home and tipping every other person you meet.

◆

Unknown Fact:

God created humans to feed mosquitos.

□

Unknown Fact:

If you always do what you always did...you will always get what you always got.

Unknown Fact:

If your parents didn't have any children... chances are, you won't have any children either.

⌘

Unknown Fact:

Guns don't Kill People. Drivers with Cell Phones Do.

○

―

Unknown Fact:

Falling on your face is still moving forward.

Unknown Fact:

Hell's Angels wear leather because Chiffon wrinkles too easily.

□

Unknown Fact:

It's illegal for women in Memphis, Tennessee to drive unless a man is in front waving a red flag to warn people and other cars.

◆

Unknown Fact:

Two can live as cheaply as one, as long as they both eat half of what they did before.

Unknown Fact:

It takes very little time for a child who is afraid of the dark to become a teenager who wants to stay out all night.

●

Unknown Fact:

More people die in bed than anywhere else.

❏

Unknown Fact:

The "golden years" was a phrase coined by someone in a nursing home holding urine samples.

❏

Unknown Fact:

Pushing the elevator button more than once does not make it arrive faster.

■

Unknown Fact:

When your kids make you angry, it will scare them more if instead of yelling, you *whisper*.

□

Unknown Fact:

Meditating...is better than sitting around doing nothing.

◆

Unknown Fact:

Massaging the back of the person in front of you at an ATM machine will help them complete their transaction faster.

⌘

Unknown Fact:

Drinking gets rid of Pimples. Not on you, but on the person you picked up at the bar.

〰

Unknown Fact:

The human brain starts working from the moment we are born and only stops when we fall in love.

⌇

Unknown Fact:

Never try to make your guests feel at home. If they wanted to feel at home, they would have stayed there.

◻

Unknown Fact:

It is a compliment if a gay guy calls you a "Dickish Delight".

⌇

Unknown Fact:

Virgin Wool comes from ugly sheep.

◻

Unknown Fact:

Technology can create a Twinkie which will last forever but a new car will only last for maybe 10 years.

Unknown Fact:

You rarely hear of someone complain about a parachute not opening.

❑

Unknown Fact:

Keeping your kid in the refrigerator for ten minutes a day, keeps them from getting "spoiled."

◆

Unknown Fact:

Absence makes the heart go wander.

Unknown Fact:

Doctors will only show X-rays to the
Kardashians after they've been retouched first.

●

Unknown Fact:

The main reason that Doctors don't write
legibly is so you don't notice their bad
spelling.

○

Unknown Fact:

You can't believe everything you hear, but
you can still repeat it.

✿

Unknown Fact:

If you make one new friend a day, in a year,
you'll be stuck with 365 new friends.

Unknown Fact:

If no one dropped out of High School, there would be no one to hire all of those College Graduates.

Unknown Fact:

Kids wouldn't like Christmas so much if they had to pay for presents.

Unknown Fact:

If someone plays Christmas music in October, you're legally allowed to kill them and use their corpse for Halloween decoration.

●

Unknown Fact:

A college professor is someone who talks while others are trying to sleep.

Unknown Fact:

You can fool some of the people all the time and all of the people some of the time, but most of the time people will make fools of themselves.

☪

"The sound of the first sip of coffee

is not much different than the sound

of an orgasm.

-Unknown

Chapter Two
Unknown Facts about:
Coffee, food and drinking

Unknown Fact:

Give a Giraffe hot coffee and it'd be cold by the time it reached the bottom of its throat.

Unknown Fact:

Americans have more food to eat than people from most countries in the world and more diets to keep them from eating it.

Unknown Fact:

Coffee is the most important meal of the day.

✿

Unknown Fact:

It is inappropriate to call the 911 operator when you run out of coffee.

♦

Unknown Fact:

There are No Winners when Corned Beef and Cabbage Farts are involved.

☺

Unknown Fact:

Unlike Milk... it's okay to cry over spilled wine.

❄

Unknown Fact:

A "Diet"... is a brief period of Starvation just prior to more weight gain.

Unknown Fact:

People who eat too many sweets often end up taking two seats.

Unknown Fact:

A refrigerator is a place where you keep leftovers until you throw them out.

()

Unknown Fact:

Married men make the best husbands.

✛

Unknown Fact:

There are only two sides to most MEN - Hungry and Horny. So, Ladies If you see your man without an erection, make him a sandwich.

□

Unknown Fact:

"Bacon"...is the drug for vegetarians.

Unknown Fact:

You can't get a hangover if you don't stop drinking.

Unknown Fact:

If you want to keep rice from sticking together...boil each grain separately.

Unknown Fact:

You can always get enough of Liver.

Unknown Fact:

Jesus fed thousands of people with One Fish and one loaf of Bread by giving them Teeny Weenie Sandwiches.

■

Unknown Fact:

Smelling food instead of eating it will help you lose weight.

⌐

Unknown Fact:

Wine helps make things not suck so much.

⊖

Unknown Fact:

Nobody likes a crooked lawyer until they need one.

◆

Unknown Fact:

The reason they call it "Fast" food is because it goes through you like a bullet.

〰

Unknown Fact:

The more you weigh, the harder it is to get kidnapped.

☒

Unknown Fact:

Every day, millions of plants are killed by vegetarians. So, help stop the violence. Eat a steak.

◻

Unknown Fact:

If you eat something and nobody sees you eat it, it has no calories.

◆

Unknown Fact:

Bacon can give men a "Lardon".

Unknown Fact:

You are a pervert if you like to eat chicken with one leg around each ear.

∿

Unknown Fact:

Lust is not real love and Taco Bell is not real Mexican food, but both are fine when you're drunk.

❐

Unknown Fact:

20 cups of coffee a day may not keep you awake, but it will help.

■

Unknown Fact:

Buffalo wings taste like chicken?

Unknown Fact:

Appetizers are those little things you eat until you lose your appetite.

Unknown Fact:

Fish...don't like the way we smell either.

Unknown Fact:

The Healthiest part of a donut is the hole.

Unknown Fact:

A fly's favorite food is Kentucky Fried Chickenshit.

Unknown Fact:

The real reason the chicken crossed the road was because Col. Sanders was chasing it.

⊖

Unknown Fact:

Decaf coffee is like sex without the sex.

✔

Unknown Fact:

If coffee, beer, wine or a nap can't cure it, you've got a serious problem.

▢

Unknown Fact:

Sex is like pizza. Even when it's not very hot...it's still good.

◼

Unknown Fact:

Every girl's dream is not to find the perfect guy. It's to eat without getting fat.

Unknown Fact:

Drinking eight glasses of beer a day is easier than drinking eight glasses of water a day.

Unknown Fact:

If you pour melted ice cream on regular ice cream, it's like a sauce.

Unknown Fact:

People drink coffee and can't sleep but most people can't drink coffee when they sleep.

Unknown Fact:

If you want to have your cake and eat it too...
buy two cakes.

◻

Unknown Fact:

Life is not a box of chocolates...it's a can of
mixed nuts.

⊖

Unknown Fact:

Vegetarians live up to nine years longer than
meat eaters. That's nine miserable bacon-less
years.

●

Unknown Fact:

The best way to enjoy a vegetable dinner is to
feed it to a cow and then eat the cow.

∎

Unknown Fact:

If coffee, beer, wine or a nap can't cure it, you've got a serious problem.

□

Unknown Fact:

Today most people don't drink coffee to wake up. They wake up to drink coffee.

❖

Unknown Fact:

Decaf coffee is like sex without the sex.

Unknown Fact:

"It takes the average teenage daughter 3 1/2 cars to learn to drive."

-Unknown

Chapter Three
More Random Unknown Facts

Unknown Fact:

A Jury is twelve people who have been chosen to decide who has the best lawyer.

❑

Unknown Fact:

A crowed elevator smells much different to a midget.

♓

Unknown Fact:

All men are animals. Some just make better pets.

♦

—

Unknown Fact:

If you always aim high, you won't pee on your shoes.

Unknown Fact:

When you argue with a fool, two fools are arguing.

Unknown Fact:

When everything's going your way, you're probably in the wrong lane.

Unknown Fact:

When surrounded, you can attack from any direction.

Unknown Fact:

When the chips are down, the buffalo is empty.

⌘

Unknown Fact:

Captain Hook died of jock itch.

◆

Unknown Fact:

The Bible was written by the same people who thought the earth was flat.

○

Unknown Fact:

Mailmen rarely go for a walk on their day off.

■

Unknown Fact:

We are all unique, just like everyone else.

——

Unknown Fact:

You should dig a hole first before having sex with a hunchback.

○

Unknown Fact:

If opportunity knocks, you still have to get up and answer the door.

Unknown Fact:

We'll all die if we live long enough.

☒

Unknown Fact:

Brain cells may come and go but fat cells last forever.

○

Unknown Fact:

The more arguments you win, the less friends you'll have.

Unknown Fact:

The more you have, the more you have to dust.

Unknown Fact:

The Indians would be better off today if they had better immigration laws.

♦

Unknown Fact:

The IRS has what it takes to take what you've got.

Unknown Fact:

The reason older people read the Bible more than young people is because they're cramming for their finals.

●

Unknown Fact:

The real reason George Washington's father did not punish him for chopping down the cherry tree was not because he didn't lie but because George still had the "ax" in his hand.

〰

Unknown Fact:

The reason Indians are no longer on the warpath is because it's been paved.

❖

Unknown Fact:

The future will be better tomorrow.

74

Unknown Fact:

"Death" was Patrick Henry's second choice.

❏

Unknown Fact:

Those who live by the sword get shot by those who don't.

■

Unknown Fact:

There are politicians who can't lie and politicians who can't tell the truth, but most can't tell the difference.

❏

Unknown Fact:

America is a place where you can say what you think without thinking.

○

Unknown Fact:

Van Gogh never needed Stereo.

●

Unknown Fact:

An apple a day keeps the doctor away, but an onion a day keeps everyone away

∾∾∾

Unknown Fact:

Gargling is the best way to tell if your throat leaks.

■

Unknown Fact:

George Washington could not throw a dollar across the Potomac today because a dollar doesn't go as far as it used to.

□

Unknown Fact:

Gay midgets come out of the cupboard.

~~~

Unknown Fact:

Today God could not create the world in six days because we have unions.

■

Unknown Fact:

Seeing a ballet is a great way to get some sleep.

□

Unknown Fact:

When you stand up for what you believe in, someone will try to steal your chair.

☒

Unknown Fact:

You can't choose your face, but you can pick your nose.

○

Unknown Fact:

Soup should be seen and not heard.

◻

Unknown Fact:

People on trial have their fate in the hands of 12 people who weren't smart enough to get out of jury duty.

〜

Unknown Fact:

"Honesty" is the fear of getting caught.

☒

Unknown Fact:

People would be healthier if they didn't get sick so much.

○

Unknown Fact:

You can keep snow from sticking to your shovel by moving to Florida.

☒

Unknown Fact:

Old people are not deaf. They've just heard everything that's worth hearing.

❑.

Unknown Fact:

Seat belts prevent people from leaving the scene of an accident.

■

Unknown Fact:

Not all lawyers are crooked. Some are dead.

Unknown Fact:

If we weren't meant to eat animals, they wouldn't be made out of meat.

Unknown Fact:

Politicians are always willing to lay down your life for their country.

Unknown Fact:

"Quit rocking the boat" was coined by Noah during mating season.

Unknown Fact:

People long for immortality when they don't even know what to do with themselves on a Sunday afternoon.

◆

Unknown Fact:

Skiers spend an arm and a leg to break an arm and a leg.

◻

Unknown Fact:

If all the world loves a lover, prostitution would be legal.

○

Unknown Fact:

If you sleep on the floor, you'll never fall out of bed.

◼

Unknown Fact:

If it's stupid and it works, it isn't stupid.

≋

Unknown Fact:

If it weren't for miracle drugs, people wouldn't be able to live long enough to pay their medical bills.

■

Unknown Fact:

The colors red, white and blue represent freedom...unless they're flashing behind your car.

□

Unknown Fact:

Egotists rarely talk about other people

■

Unknown Fact:

A naked man jogging is also a swinger.

Unknown Fact:

Short people are always the last ones to know when it rains.

♦

Unknown Fact:

If it weren't for the last minute, nothing would get done.

○

Unknown Fact:

When you moo to a cow, the cow will not moo back.

■

Unknown Fact:

It's better to have loved and lost than to have to do homework with your kids every night.

Unknown Fact:

It's lonely at the top, but you eat much better.

❖

Unknown Fact:

It's hard to make a comeback when you haven't been anywhere.

❑

Unknown Fact:

You should never invest your money in anything that eats.

■

Unknown Fact:

It doesn't do any good spanking a teen-ager, but it can be fun.

○

Unknown Fact:

It's always darkest before daylight savings time.

□

Unknown Fact:

Youth is wasted on children.

○

Unknown Fact:

If you raise your hands to your kids, it leaves your groin unprotected.

■

Unknown Fact:

The time it takes to fold a fitted sheet is between 10 and 20 minutes.

Unknown Fact:

New Year's resolutions usually go in one year and out the other.

❖

Unknown Fact:

News is the same thing happening today that happened yesterday, only to different people.

■

Unknown Fact:

The person who said, "All you need is Love" already had everything that money could buy.

◆

Unknown Fact:

If you race a train to a crossing and it's a tie, you lose.

□

Unknown Fact:

If you plant tomatoes in warm asphalt, they will not grow.

◮

Unknown Fact:

The meaning of life is in the dictionary.

◫

Unknown Fact:

If you take a nap in your fireplace, you'll sleep like a log.

■

Unknown Fact:

In Hollywood, virgins can be recognized by out of town plates.

❑

Unknown Fact:

If you put a girl on a pedestal, you can see under her dress.

∿

Unknown Fact:

It's better to be over the hill than under it.

○

Unknown Fact:

It was Donald Duck who said, "A quack is just a pwace to put a pwick".

●

Unknown Fact:

There is no such thing as a recipe for left over bacon.

Unknown Fact:

If your dog licks your face, it's to get the taste of his ass out of its mouth.

Unknown Fact:

If it weren't for "venetian blinds"... it'd be "curtains" for all of us.

Unknown Fact:

The truth will set you free... but first it will piss you off.

Unknown Fact:

Only one in ten people actually "jump" in the shower.

○

Unknown Fact:

Stupid people do not know they're stupid.

■

Unknown Fact:

If a dog breaks a mirror, it will have 49 years of bad luck.

□

Unknown Fact:

It takes over 10 minutes for a giraffe to throw up.

□

Unknown Fact:

Brown colored toilet paper does not exist.

~~~

Unknown Fact:

A camel with one hump can go four months without water, but a man, no matter how much water you give him... cannot go four months without a hump.

◿

Unknown Fact:

Food always tastes better when someone else makes it.

□

Unknown Fact:

Donuts are just an excuse to eat cake in the morning.

Unknown Fact:

There's more graffiti in a ladies room than there is in a men's room because they get to use both hands.

Unknown Fact:

When you resist temptation, you'll feel happiness but if you give in to it... you'll feel greater happiness.

❖

Unknown Fact:

Immature is what boring people call those who like to have fun.

〰

Unknown Fact:

Saying we can still be friends is like saying the dog died but you can keep it.

○

Unknown Fact:

Some mistakes happen for a reason, but most mistakes happen because people are stupid.

■

Unknown Fact:

Condoms prevent minivans.

□

Unknown Fact:

The real reason they're called "Cell" phones is because people are prisoners of them.

■

Unknown Fact:

You can't fix stupid, but you can still laugh at it.

●

Unknown Fact:

You can only say, "My god, look at you. You got so big" to children.

○

Unknown Fact:

If you don't fart, the gas will travel up your spine and into your brain and that's where shitty ideas come from.

〜

Unknown Fact:

It's not the thought that counts, but the gift behind it.

▫

Unknown Fact:

If there's enough room to spell "Bootylicious" on the back of your shorts, it probably isn't.

□

Unknown Fact:

If you love someone, let them go. If they come back, no one else wanted them.

●

Unknown Fact:

If you can't fix it with duct tape, you're not using enough duct tape.

❏

Unknown Fact:

A speaker at a cremation service is also known as a "Toastmaster".

■

Unknown Fact:

It's easier to stay up until 6 am than to wake up at 6 am.

❑

Unknown Fact:

If there's a shortcut, someone else has probably already taken it.

◻

Unknown Fact:

Unless life also gives you water and sugar, that lemonade is going to suck.

◼

Unknown Fact:

You can't buy happiness...but you can buy bacon and that's damn close.

○

Unknown Fact:

There's more to life than money. There's also credit cards, stocks, bonds, gold, jewelry and diamonds.

Unknown Fact:

More people will sit at a stop sign and wait for it to turn green on Monday mornings.

Unknown Fact:

You can't say "good eye might" without sounding Australian.

Unknown Fact:

People spend more money on Mother's Day than on Father's Day.

⊠

Unknown Fact:

If you're not confused...you're not well informed.

♒

Unknown Fact:

Santa has the same wrapping paper as most parents.

◻

Unknown Fact:

If your phone gets wet, put it in rice overnight. During the night, the rice will attract Asians who will then fix it.

☒

Unknown Fact:

If you close your eyes and turn on your TV, it's just like radio.

○

Unknown Fact:

George Washington is the only President who didn't blame his problems on the previous administration.

❑

Unknown Fact:

The things that come to those who wait will be the things left by those who got there first.

〰

Unknown Fact:

A dog can't be trusted to watch your food.

■

Unknown Fact:

Pressing harder on a remote control when the batteries are dead doesn't make it work better.

●

Unknown Fact:

You have a drinking problem if your idea of Frozen Food is Scotch on the Rocks.

●

Unknown Fact:

Nothing messes up a Friday more than realizing it's actually Wednesday.

○

Unknown Fact:

You will always win at the race track if you bet more money on the winners than on the losers.

〰

Unknown Fact:

It's impossible to get to work at 8 a.m. if you leave your house at 8:01 a.m.

⌘

Unknown Fact:

An education is what's left over after you subtract what you forgot from what you learned.

●

Unknown Fact:

6 out of 7 dwarfs are not Happy.

〰️

Unknown Fact:

Politicians didn't invent crime. They just improved on it.

●

Unknown Fact:

Texas has miles and miles of miles and miles.

○

Unknown Fact:

You can't eat your cake and diet too.

●

Unknown Fact:

The best way to solve a parking problem is to buy a parked car.

☒

Unknown Fact:

A psychiatrist does not believe in the phrase, "A penny for your thoughts."

●

Unknown Fact:

If the earth began rotating 30 times faster than normal, workers would get their monthly pay check every day and would women bleed to death.

☐

Unknown Fact:

The first plane invented in the early 1900's did not ever get off the ground and was built by the "Wrong Brothers".

∿

Unknown Fact:

If you see conjoined twins fighting, you should never try to separate them.

■

Unknown Fact:

A miracle teenager once survived on his own for almost six hours with no Wi Fi.

■

Unknown Fact:

Headaches are all in your head.

❑

Unknown Fact:

People who are afraid of Santa Claus are Claustrophobic.

◆

Unknown Fact:

Italian foreplay...is whistling.

■

Unknown Fact:

The best time to buy a used car is when it's new.

○

Unknown Fact:

The first five days after the weekend are the hardest.

〰

Unknown Fact:

Moby Dick... is not a venereal disease.

———

Unknown Fact:

It's easier to eat oysters if you take them out of the shell first.

■

Unknown Fact:

The grass may be greener on the other side... but their water bill is much higher.

●

Unknown Fact:

After a haircut, your hearing gets better until your next haircut.

☒

Unknown Fact:

Getting a vasectomy at "Supercuts" is not a good idea.

◆

Unknown Fact:

Mohair does not come from a guy named Moe.

□

Unknown Fact:

Exercise is good for killing germs but getting germs to exercise is next to impossible.

○

Unknown Fact:

A friend in need is a friend to stay away from.

●

Unknown Fact:

Christmas is a time when neither the past nor the future is as important as the "Present".

●

Unknown Fact:

The more birthdays you have, the longer you'll live.

□

Chapter Four
Unknown Facts about:
Men, Women, and Sex

Unknown Fact:

Eve slept with the first man she met.

≋

Unknown Fact:

A bachelor can get out of bed from either side.

□

Unknown Fact:

A beautiful woman does not have to be as great in bed as an ugly woman does.

◐

Unknown Fact:

You'll never know if you like bathing beauties until you bathe one.

●

Unknown Fact:

Women can never change a man, unless he's in diapers.

◻

Unknown Fact:

Your wife finding a letter you forgot to mail is not as bad as your wife finding a letter you forgot to burn.

♒

Unknown Fact:

A good woman is good, but a bad woman is better.

◻

Unknown Fact:

Arguing with a woman is like reading the software license agreement. In the end you ignore everything and click..."I agree".

~~~

Unknown Fact:

A lesbian is just another woman trying to do a man's job.

●

Unknown Fact:

Everyone who is in favor of birth control has already been born.

~~~

Unknown Fact:

Alimony is the screwing you get for the screwing you got.

□

Unknown Fact:

All men are animals. Some just make better pets.

□

Unknown Fact:

A man who fights with his wife during the day, gets no "piece" at night.

■

Unknown Fact:

A Man with 10 million dollars is no happier than a man with 9 million dollars.

○

Unknown Fact:

A man should always look both ways before crossing a street or a woman.

〰

Unknown Fact:

We are born wet, naked and hungry... then it gets worse.

■

Unknown Fact:

A man who thinks he is smarter than his wife has a very smart wife.

□

Unknown Fact:

A man chases a woman until she catches him.

○

Unknown Fact:

The reason women it's difficult for women to find men who are caring, sensitive and good looking is because they already have boyfriends.

●

Unknown Fact:

The worst thing about having sex with a cow
is you have to walk around to kiss it.

☒

Unknown Fact:

Beauty isn't everything, but it sure is nice to
look at.

〰

Unknown Fact:

There are lots of things you can't say with
flowers.

○

Unknown Fact:

The 10 best years of a woman's life are
between 29 and 30.

●

Unknown Fact:

Arguing with a woman is like trying to read a newspaper in a hurricane.

❏

Unknown Fact:

A virgin is a girl who hasn't yet met her maker.

●

Unknown Fact:

A woman always has the last word in any argument. Anything a man says after that is the beginning of a new argument.

↗

Unknown Fact:

A woman gives sex to get love and a man gives love to get sex.

☒

Unknown Fact:

A woman is just as beautiful at forty as she was at twenty. It just takes longer.

●

Unknown Fact:

The best oral contraceptive is still the word, "No".

○

Unknown Fact:

The quickest way to a man's heart is to split open his breast plate with an "Ax".

□

Unknown Fact:

The first thing a man should do after winning an argument with his wife is apologize.

▪

Unknown Fact:

Dutch prostitutes are better because they'll pay half.

●

Unknown Fact:

"For better or worse" really means the bride couldn't do any better and the groom couldn't do any worse.

○

Unknown Fact:

For men, the first day on a nude beach is the hardest.

■

Unknown Fact:

Girls may lose their virginity, but they still get to keep the box it came in.

□

Unknown Fact:

If you give a girl 2 drinks, she'll feel it. If you give her 4 drinks, you'll feel it.

~~~

Unknown Fact:

God created the orgasm so we would all know when to stop.

⌘

Unknown Fact:

It's impossible to have sex standing up in a canoe.

❏

Unknown Fact:

Some women count on their fingers but most count on their tits and ass.

~~~

Unknown Fact:

Husbands wouldn't lie so much if women would stop asking so many questions.

⌘

Unknown Fact:

It costs a fortune for women to look cheap.

☒

Unknown Fact:

A Eunuch is someone who is cut off from temptation.

◼

Unknown Fact:

A widow always knows where her husband is.

◖

"Men who go bald in the front are lovers, men who go bald in the back are thinkers, men who go bald all over think they're lovers."

- Unknown

Unknown Fact:

People who marry for money usually earn every penny of it.

≈

Unknown Fact:

You will always think of great things you shoulda said within two minutes after an argument.

■

Unknown Fact:

Women spend more time thinking about what men are thinking than men spend thinking.

❑

Unknown Fact:

Sex is not a four-letter word.

≈

Unknown Fact:

If you have sex with a prostitute while she's sleeping, it's stealing.

○

Unknown Fact:

Arguing with a woman is like getting arrested. Anything you say can and will be used against you.

◻

Unknown Fact:

Sex is the most fun you can have without laughing.

❑

Unknown Fact:

If you can't remember her name in the morning, bring her to Starbucks.

○

Unknown Fact:

The best way for men to avoid arguments with women about leaving the toilet seat up is to use the sink.

□

Unknown Fact:

When you're at someone's home you're dating for the first time, you will suddenly have to poop.

〰

Unknown Fact:

Women frequently can't find their purse, lipstick or car keys but Can always remember something you said 9 months ago.

□

Unknown Fact:

The only people who have sex every night are liars.

~~~

Unknown Fact:

The less there is of a woman's bathing suit, the more it costs.

○

Unknown Fact:

People who sleep like a baby have never had one.

●

Unknown Fact:

Men may wear the pants in a relationship... but women control the zipper.

❏

Unknown Fact:

Liza Minnelli...is a sex symbol for men who no longer care.

■

Unknown Fact:

One good turn gets most of the covers.

□

Unknown Fact:

If a guy remembers the color of a woman's eyes after a first date... chances are she has small boobs?

〜

Unknown Fact:

The best kind of birth control is often just Good Lighting.

❏

Unknown Fact:

Incest is okay as long as it's kept in the family.

※

Unknown Fact:

If a man doesn't bring his wife flowers, she gets mad. If he does bring her flowers, she gets suspicious.

○

Unknown Fact:

Three's company but eight is definitely an orgy.

■

Unknown Fact:

A couple has never been found who got married and lived happily ever after.

※

Unknown Fact:

If a Man comes home early, she thinks he wants something. If he comes home late, she thinks he's already had it.

◻

Unknown Fact:

No matter how many hours you sleep, when you wake up, you need 5 more minutes of sleep.

▪

Unknown Fact:

Women want "one" man to satisfy her "every" need and men want "every" woman to satisfy his "one" need.

〰

Unknown Fact:

The weaker sex is the stronger sex because of the weakness of the stronger sex for the weaker sex.

○

Unknown Fact:

Men socialize by insulting each other, but they don't really mean it. Women socialize by complimenting each other, but they don't really mean it.

●

Unknown Fact:

If a man has 5 wives, 4 have it pretty soft.

◻

Unknown Fact:

If at first you don't succeed, you should try foreplay.

Unknown Fact:

It's not premarital sex if you never get married.

●

Unknown Fact:

When a guy is horny, his wife or girlfriend is always right.

◻

Unknown Fact:

Without a Marriage license, you can't get a divorce.

〜

Unknown Fact:

"Making Love" is what women do while men are fucking them.

❏

Unknown Fact:

Women who are friendly, co-operative and good sports are likely to have lots of kids.

◻

Unknown Fact:

Marriage is a relationship in which one person is always right and the other is a husband.

●

Unknown Fact:

When a man says, "Ladies First"... it's just a nice way of him saying, "Let me check out your ass while you walk in front of me."

○

Unknown Fact:

Women spend more time wondering what men are thinking than men spend thinking.

♒

Unknown Fact:

The number one sign that a woman really loves a man is if she'll have sex with him right after She's had her hair done.

≋

Unknown Fact:

If you turn on Women's Tennis and shut your eyes, it sounds a lot like porn.

●

Unknown Fact:

Dating after 60 is like riding a bike: two flat tires, the frame is busted, the chain doesn't move and one of the pedals is missing.

❑

Unknown Fact:

The best way to avoid Sex is to get married.

■

Unknown Fact:

A widow and her money are soon married.

□

Unknown Fact:

You should always dig a hole first before having sex with a hunchback.

○

Unknown Fact:

If a Kardashian woman shits in the woods...they'll figure a way to make money off it.

●

Unknown Fact:

The most dangerous year in a marriage is the First...then the Second, then the third, the fourth and so on and so on.

○

Unknown Fact:

Marriage is the number one cause of divorce.

◻

Unknown Fact:

God gave women "nipples" to make "suckers" out of Men.

●

Unknown Fact:

When a woman is mad, telling her she is overreacting will cause her to immediately calm down. (NOT)

●

Unknown Fact:

Husbands are the best people to share your secrets with. They'll never tell anyone because they're not even listening.

≋

Unknown Fact:

It's not unlucky to postpone a wedding as long as you keep on doing it.

○

Unknown Fact:

Women have PMS because men have ESPN.

⌘

Unknown Fact:

The reason most women are bad at parking is because they're constantly lied to about what 8 inches looks like.

☒

Unknown Fact:

The reason it takes more than a million male sperm to fertilize one female egg is because not one will stop and ask for directions.

☐

Unknown Fact:

People who live in glass houses should always fuck in the basement.

〰

Unknown Fact:

Men are basically just a life-support system for their penis.

☐

Unknown Fact:

Men are all alike but have different faces so you can tell them apart.

●

Unknown Fact:

You can tell a lot about a woman's mood by her hands. If they are holding a gun, she's probably mad.

〰

Unknown Fact:

Marrying for money is better than marrying for no reason at all.

⌘

Unknown Fact:

When couples get married, it's the lawyers who live happily ever after.

◼

Unknown Fact:

Girls take vitamin pills to get into shape and birth control pills to stay that way.

◯

Unknown Fact:

Underneath every successful man, there's a woman.

□

Unknown Fact:

Getting married in your early twenties is like leaving a party before ten.

■

Unknown Fact:

Sex is like chess. There's a lot of moves but the ending is always the same.

□

Unknown Fact:

When a woman says that she loves you from the bottom of her heart, that could mean there's room at the top for others.

〰

Unknown Fact:

The best way for a man to meet available women is to become a divorce lawyer.

□

Unknown Fact:

A woman saying, "I'm not mad at you" is like a dentist saying "You won't feel a thing."

■

Unknown Fact:

You can tell a lot about a woman by the way she slashes your tires.

□

Unknown Fact:

Men like to insult each other, but they don't mean it. Women like to complement each other, and they don't mean it either.

●

Unknown Fact:

A woman saying, "I'll be ready in 5 minutes."
and a man saying, "I'll be home in 5 minutes."
are exactly the same.

●

Unknown Fact:

When three women are talking, you have
conversation. When one leaves, you have
gossip.

〰

Unknown Fact:

The sight of a woman's naked breasts causes
a man to lose his ability to think clearly by
50%...per boob.

○

"There are more smart phones than smart people."

- **Unknown**

Unknown Fact:

Men will never find a woman who will love them the way women in commercials love yogurt.

○

Unknown Fact:

The time taken by a wife when she says I'll be ready in 5 minutes is equal to the time taken by a husband when he says I'll call you in 5 minutes.

〰

Unknown Fact:

Women cannot apply mascara with their mouths closed.

●

Unknown Fact:

If you are married to someone who snores, they will always fall asleep first.

❏

Unknown Fact:

If you watch porn upside down... it doesn't look any different.

☐

Unknown Fact:

The real meaning of PMS...prepare to meet Satan.

●

Unknown Fact:

Women fake orgasms because men fake foreplay.

○

Unknown Fact:

The reason women will never propose to men is because as soon as they get on their knees, the guy will start unzipping.

❑

Unknown Fact:

Girls today are not what they were 20 years ago because they're 20 years older.

❑

Unknown Fact:

The key to a woman's heart is laughter - unless she's laughing at your penis.

⌘

Unknown Fact:

Men have friends with benefits, but women have friends with batteries.

☒

Unknown Fact:

If you can fool "One" of the people all the time, you'll have a successful marriage.

~~

Unknown Fact:

It takes 235 muscles to fake an orgasm but only ten muscles to say, "It's a clitoris and it's right here."

◻

Unknown Fact:

Some women are easy to look at... while others close their curtains.

◯

Unknown Fact:

The one thing that men and women in common is...they both don't trust women.

☒

Unknown Fact:

Women mature much faster than men because Men don't get boobs 'til they're in their fifties and sixties.

●

Unknown Fact:

Women are right even when they are wrong.

♒

Unknown Fact:

The most common marriage proposal is still...
"You're going to have a WHAT?"

⌘

Unknown Fact:

Women always have the last word except when talking to another woman.

♐

Unknown Fact:

No man has ever been shot by his wife while he was doing the dishes.

□

Unknown Fact:

Women love men in uniform because they know how to follow orders.

□

Unknown Fact:

The average amount of time a woman can keep a secret is 11 hours and 16 minutes.

●

Unknown Fact:

You should never ask a woman who is eating ice cream straight from the carton how she's doing.

□

Unknown Fact:

Adam was the first Man to say "Stand back. I don't know how big this thing is going to get."

❑

Unknown Fact:

The pill is the second-best thing a girl can put in her mouth to avoid pregnancy.

●

Unknown Fact:

When a woman nags you, that is a sign she cares. When a woman is silent, that is a sign she's plotting your death.

○

Unknown Fact:

Vaginas have an On and Off switch linked to the words that come out of a man's mouth.

❑

"When signing a contract, the large print gives it away... and the small print takes it away."

- Unknown

Unknown Fact:

Today, if you want a virgin, you need to be there when they come out.

□

Unknown Fact:

A girl never chases after a guy unless he's trying to get away.

■

Unknown Fact:

There are 3 sizes of condoms...Small, Medium and Liar.

❑

Unknown Fact:

It's better to be the second husband of a widow than the first.

○

Unknown Fact:

What women really want is for their man to drag them to the bedroom, throw them on the bed, then clean the house while they take a nap.

○

Unknown Fact:

Today, if you want a virgin, you need to be there when they come out.

□

Unknown Fact:

Nobody cleans a house faster than a guy expecting sex.

○

Unknown Fact:

When a man is quiet, he is thinking... When a woman is quiet, she is pissed.

Unknown Fact:

Women's minds are cleaner than Men's because they change them more often.

○

Unknown Fact:

The best way to get over someone... is to get Under someone else.

◻

Unknown Fact:

Women with huge butts live longer than men who mention it.

●

Unknown Fact:

If a woman grabs a man by the balls, his heart and mind will soon follow.

〜〜
〜〜

Unknown Fact:

Most people prefer Valentine's night to Valentine's Day.

□

Unknown Fact:

There's a fine line between cuddling and holding someone down so they can't get away.

●

Unknown Fact:

There's nothing better than the love of a good woman unless it's the love of a bad woman.

□

Unknown Fact:

You can't buy love, but you can still pay a hell of a lot for it.

○

Unknown Fact:

Telling your wife you're leaving her for someone else is one of those things you "Can't" say with flowers.

●

Unknown Fact:

The reason sex is so popular is because it's centrally located.

○

Unknown Fact:

If a woman likes you she'll let you but if she loves you, she'll help you.

〰

Unknown Fact:

"LIFE"... is a sexually transmitted disease.

☐

Unknown Fact:

For most women, Life is an endless struggle, full of frustration and challenges... until they find a Hair Stylist they like.

〜〜

Unknown Fact:

Adam was the first person to turn over a new leaf.

☒

Unknown Fact:

Early to bed and Early to rise makes a man healthy, wealthy and boring.

●

Unknown Fact:

It takes balls for a transvestite to walk into a Men's room.

Unknown Fact:

Women spend half their money on food and the other half trying to lose weight.

○

Unknown Fact:

Sex is the one thing that takes the least amount of time yet causes the most amount of trouble.

●

Unknown Fact:

Men come home "half loaded" because they ran out of money.

☒

Unknown Fact:

A girl in the hand is better than just the Hand.

☒

Unknown Fact:

Men should never underestimate a woman unless they're talking about her age or her weight.

❑

Unknown Fact:

A man can tell by a woman's thighs if she likes him. If one is on each side of his head, she likes him.

⌘

Unknown Fact:

Sex is like a Broadway play. If nobody comes, it's a flop.

◯

Unknown Fact:

A "Conscience" is that little something that prompts a man to tell his wife something bad he's done before someone else does.

□

Unknown Fact:

"Oral Sex"...is the sincerest form of flattery.

○

Unknown Fact:

Women are like paper clips. You often have too many of them or none at all.

●

Unknown Fact:

Women believe in Love at First Sight. Men believe in at First Opportunity.

●

Unknown Fact:

God made man before woman so as to give him time to think of an answer before her first question.

❑

Unknown Fact:

There are two ways to argue with a woman and neither one work.

"There are three kinds of people in the world. Those who are good at Math and those who aren't."

- Unknown

Chapter Five:

Unknown Facts about:

Math, Stats and Percentages

Unknown Fact:

9 out of 10 times when you think to yourself, "I don't need to write that down. I'll remember it." you will not remember it.

❑

Unknown Fact:

100% of the time when you offer someone bacon. they'll take it.

■

Unknown Fact:

Over 50% of men who graduate from college want to marry a woman with a steady job.

◻

Unknown Fact:

3 out of 4 times when you think the dishes are done, you'll turn around and see you still have a bunch of pots left on the stove.

◼

Unknown Fact:

Supermarkets use 5 or 6 checkout stands out of 8...unless it's really busy, then they use 2.

♒

Unknown Fact:

Over 98% of people have never used algebra after leaving school.

◻

Unknown Fact:

When you have a 50/50 chance of getting something right 90% of the time you will be wrong.

●

Unknown Fact:

3 out of 4 times when your significant other rushes you to get ready, when you are, they won't be.

☒

Unknown Fact:

9 out of 10 times when you go to a huge sale at a store, everything will be on sale except what you want to buy.

☐

Unknown Fact:

Over 90% of adults have a plastic bag full of plastic bags in the pantry.

❏

Unknown Fact:

10% of blonde women fake an orgasm with their vibrator.

〰

Unknown Fact:

9 out of 10 times when people say, "Just a Second'... it will be at least 5 minutes

☒

Unknown Fact:

50% of the time when you spit out your car window, the window will be closed.

■

Unknown Fact:

3 out of 4 times when you go to high five someone, you will miss.

•

Unknown Fact:

60% of people who fail their driving tests become valet parking attendants.

□

Unknown Fact:

One dollar bill out of every 10,000 was once in a Stripper's Crack.

○

Unknown Fact:

50% of the time, when you buy popcorn at the movies, you will end up eating all the popcorn before the movie has started.

■

Unknown Fact:

3 out of 4 times when you bite into a chocolate chip cookie, you'll find out they're raisins.

᷈

Unknown Fact:

When you're in your car picking your nose, 9 out of 10 times, the person in the car next to you looking at you.

☐

Unknown Fact:

If Caitlyn Jenner ever got lost, her picture will be put on carton of half and half.

○

Unknown Fact:

9 out of 10 times when there are 5 lines at the supermarket, you will get into the slowest one.

□

Unknown Fact:

We don't get any smarter when we get older. We just run out of stupid shit to do.

〰

Unknown Fact:

10% of heroes were really cowards who ran the wrong way.

□

Unknown Fact:

9 out of 10 times when someone is being nice to you, it's because they want something from you.

Unknown Fact:

50% of the time, when you try to pull your blanket up, you will punch yourself in the face.

□

Unknown Fact:

9 out of 10 times women forget to put the seat UP after they're finished.

■

Unknown Fact:

70% of men with testicular cancer blame it on women who smoke.

□

Unknown Fact:

9 out of 10 times, your kid will sneak up on you while you're watching porn.

○

Unknown Fact:

3 out of 4 times when you go out with friends for coffee, you will get back home stinking drunk.

≋

Unknown Fact:

3 out of 4 times when people say, "I Swear to God it's the truth," it's not.

■

Unknown Fact:

Golf is a long walk broken up by swearing, disappointment and bad math.

≋

Unknown Fact:

Over 50% of kids who don't come when you call them become waiters.

❑

Unknown Fact:

9 out of 10 times, when you rush for some bug killer for a spider you saw on the wall, when you get back, it will no longer be there.

≈

Unknown Fact:

3 out of 4 times when you make a list before going to the grocery store, when you get there, you'll realize you forgot to bring it.

◻

Unknown Fact:

10% of mothers have kissed their kids goodnight after giving their husbands a blowjob.

▪

Unknown Fact:

Half of marriages end in divorce...the other half fight it out to the bitter end.

□

Unknown Fact:

3 out of 4 times when you get comfortable on the sofa, your significant other will yell for you to do something.

○

Unknown Fact:

A human body is worth 98 cents, but a cow's body is worth over $2,000 dollars. (think about that)

■

Unknown Fact:

50% of vacuum cleaners sit in a closet gathering dust.

Unknown Fact:

9 out of 10 times when you think to yourself, "I don't need to write that down. I'll remember it." you will not remember it.

■

Unknown Fact:

80% of men and only 10% of women love playing "how long can I drive with my-gas-light-on?"

○

Unknown Fact:

60% of Americans think that beauty is on the inside of a fridge.

●

Unknown Fact:

The only things you really can count on are your fingers.

Unknown Fact:

A 2-pound box of candy will put 10 pounds on a woman.

○

Unknown Fact:

80% of Americans will be able to retire 10 years after they die.

□

Unknown Fact:

9 out of 10 times when you think you hear opportunity knocking, it will turn out to be a Jehovah's witness.

■

"3 out of 4 times when you do something awesome, no one will see it, but when you do something embarrassing, everyone will see it."

-Unknown

Unknown Fact:

30% of married women say their cat is a better listener than their husband. 70% of cats say these crazy women need to shut up.

□

Unknown Fact:

9 out of 10 times when you hold the door open for someone, everybody in the building decides to go out.

〰

Unknown Fact:

75% of men look for brains in a woman... after they've looked at everything else.

■

Unknown Fact:

9 out of 10 times when a package says easy to open, you will have to use a knife, scissors, screwdriver and/or chainsaw to open it.

○

Unknown Fact:

Keeping at least 500 dollars in your savings account is like having money in the bank.

♒

Unknown Fact:

If you take your age and add 5 to it. That is your age in 5 years.

○

Unknown Fact:

98% of people like getting gifts more than giving them.

Unknown Fact:

Most people's hands measure 9 inches. Three
more inches and it would be a foot.

~~~

Unknown Fact:

In a courtroom it takes a jury of 12 to
determine if a woman is innocent. In a bar it
takes 3 to 5 drinks to find if a woman is
innocent.

❏

Unknown Fact:

50% of men keep their eyes open when
kissing to see if their wives are around.

◯

Unknown Fact:

3 out of 4 times when you're waiting to scare your friend, they will take forever to come out.

■

Unknown Fact:

99% of women will admit they're right if you admit you're wrong.

□

Unknown Fact:

9 out of 10 times when people want to whisper a secret to you in your ear, they will have bad breath.

○

Unknown Fact:

50% of the time, when you're riding your bike, you will get hit by a parked car.

●

Unknown Fact:

50% of the time, when you finish wrapping a present, you will leave the price tag on.

□

Unknown Fact:

3 out of 4 times when you do something awesome, no one will see it, but when you do something embarrassing, everyone will see it.

▩

Unknown Fact:

3 out of 4 people make up 75% of the world's population.

Unknown Fact:

The 3 ways women stay Young are:1) Dieting 2) Exercising 3) Lying about their age.

●

Unknown Fact:

9 out of 10 times, when you ask a woman when the baby's due, they're not pregnant. (Always wait until you see a leg or arm hanging out first).

□

Unknown Fact:

Death is the number one killer in the world.

〜

Unknown Fact:

100% of the people reading this are alive.

○

Unknown Fact:

98% of the time that pen you let that person borrow won't be returned.

●

Unknown Fact:

20% of kids use the same bar of soap to wash their face that their dad washed his balls with.

〰〰

Unknown Fact:

9 out of 10 times when you yawn in front of a friend, they will stick their finger in your mouth mid yawn.

☐

Unknown Fact:

The ingredients in Viagra are 2% aspirin, 8% starch and 90% fix a flat.

Unknown Fact: The easiest way to find something you lost around the house is to buy a replacement.

Chapter Six
Yet Even More Random
Unknown Facts

Unknown Fact:

The reason so many people act like assholes is because it's so easy.

❏

Unknown Fact:

The world isn't really worse off... there's just better news coverage.

〰

Unknown Fact:

There was once a Patriotic Porno film called, "Yank my Doodle it's a dandy".

▓

Unknown Fact:

Doctors performed their first penis transplant on a man in 1988. Unfortunately, six months later his right hand rejected it.

~~~

Unknown Fact:

Ford once invented a car made completely out of wood. It had a wooden body, a wooden engine and wooden wheels but they couldn't sell it because it wooden go.

❑

Unknown Fact:

When you put something in a safe place so you don't lose it, you will later forget where that safe place is.

●

Unknown Fact:

A golf ball is something you chase when you're too old to chase women.

■

Unknown Fact:

No matter how amazing you are at something, there will always be an eight-year old Asian who is better.

□

Unknown Fact:

When signing a contract, the large print gives it away... and the small print takes it away.

●

Unknown Fact:

Laugh and the world laughs with you but if you fart, you fart alone.

☒

Unknown Fact:

If they served parishioners on Sunday morning during church services, they'd have more people showing up.

Unknown Fact:

"Men do not "win" arguments with their wives, they "survive" them.

●

Unknown Fact:

Hollywood is the only place where people Drive three blocks to go work out at the gym.

○

Unknown Fact:

If pigs could fly, their wings would taste delicious.

〰

Unknown Fact:

If you teach a child to be polite and courteous, when they grow up, they'll never be able to merge their car onto the freeway

~~~

Unknown Fact:

Some people can't sleep because they have insomnia, but most people can't sleep because they have an internet connection.

■

Unknown Fact:

When one door closes, another one opens...or you can just open the closed door.

Unknown Fact:

Most people don't need religion as long as they have wine.

Unknown Fact:

A doctor can bury his mistakes, an architect can cover his mistakes , but a teacher's mistakes eventually grow up and become lawyers.

●

Unknown Fact:

Artificial intelligence is no match for natural stupidity.

☒

Unknown Fact:

"Later"... is the best time to do most things.

∿

Unknown Fact:

The normal mortality rate in the U.S. averages about one per person.

○

Unknown Fact:

The amount of time between throwing something away and then needing it, is about two days.

■

Unknown Fact:

If it seems easy, you're doing it wrong.

□

Unknown Fact:

More people would exercise if was as easy as eating.

●

Unknown Fact:

Taking candy from a baby is not really that hard.

♒

Unknown Fact:

When a Pit Bull is licking you, he's not being friendly...he's basting you.

●

Unknown Fact:

If your prayers aren't answered, the answer is No.

○

Unknown Fact:

Gasoline and whiskey actually DO mix but it tastes terrible.

◻

Unknown Fact:

Assholes do not know that they're assholes.

〰

Unknown Fact:

Giraffes do NOT know what farts smell like.

❑

Unknown Fact:

The first two minutes of life are very dangerous... and so are the last two minutes.

⌘

Unknown Fact:

Pleasing everyone is impossible...but pissing everyone off is easy and fun.

〰

Unknown Fact:

Telling people who are assholes that they are assholes can add up to 3 years to your life.

●

"If all the politicians in America were laid end to end... that'd be okay with most people."

- **Unknown Fact**

Unknown Fact:

Bats are the only living thing that can hang upside down without shitting on themselves.

◻

Unknown Fact:

The sole purpose of a child's middle name is so he can tell when he's really in trouble.

■

Unknown Fact:

Anything is possible...if you

don't know what you are talking about.

〜

Unknown Fact:

The less you have... the more there is to get.

❏

Unknown Fact:

It's called "work" because if it was fun, it would be called "fun".

●

Unknown Fact:

You can accidently make a baby, but you can't accidently make a pizza.

○

Unknown Fact:

Sharp knives have been linked to penis shrinkage.

■

Unknown Fact:

Whenever you're holding all the right cards, everyone wants to play chess.

○

Unknown Fact:

It's much easier getting older than getting wiser.

♒

Unknown Fact:

Happiness comes from within... which is why it feels good to fart.

☒

Unknown Fact:

Indian Chief "Sitting Bull" had a gay brother named, "Sitting Pretty"

○

Unknown Fact:

The Incas had no word for Styrofoam.

●

Unknown Fact:

Horses are banned from restaurants in Japan, not because they are animals, but because they take too long to remove their shoes.

❏

Unknown Fact:

Bells were originally put on Cows to keep them from catching birds.

■

Unknown Fact:

No moth has ever been accused of being gay for coming out of the closet.

☒

Unknown Fact:

A parking space will automatically disappear when you make a U-Turn.

■

Unknown Fact:

It was the Mexican people who first figured out that laundering clothes by beating them against rocks worked fine and the Polish people who learned that same method wasn't great for washing dishes.

○

Unknown Fact:

A California man paid a fine for deliberately driving his golden retriever puppy insane by naming it "Fetch".

■

Unknown Fact:

George Washington's teeth were made of wood and at night before retiring he would place them in a glass of lemon pledge.

〰

Unknown Fact:

Calcium is good for your teeth, but minding your own business is even better.

■

Unknown Fact:

Robin Hood robbed from the rich because the poor had no money.

❑

Unknown Fact:

If you have a cough, take large doses of laxatives, then you'll be afraid to cough.

〰

Unknown Fact:

The first lie detector was made out of a rib from man...no improvement has ever been made on the original.

○

Unknown Fact:

When Muslim female suicide bombers die, they get 72 sensitive and caring single men who'll listen to them and remember their anniversary.

■

Unknown Fact:

If you took out all the veins from your body and laid them end to end, you would die.

○

Unknown Fact:

If you help someone when they're in trouble, they'll always remember you, especially the next time they're in trouble.

☒

Unknown Fact:

The best way to cure Insomnia... is to get lots of sleep.

■

Unknown Fact:

You could die if you get scared half to death twice.

❑

Unknown Fact:

People who are closed minded should be closed mouthed as well.

○

Unknown Fact:

"Wino" is not the opposite of "Why Yes".

■

Unknown Fact:

It's not hard to meet expenses. They're everywhere.

Unknown Fact:

People who say sticks and stones can break my bones but words will never hurt me have most likely never been hit with a dictionary.

〜

Unknown Fact:

Counting sheep doesn't help people who are excited by sheep.

❏

Unknown Fact:

It's better to have loved and lost than to live with a psycho for the rest of your life.

■

Unknown Fact:

Ping Pong Balls is not a form of Chinese V.D.

⌘

Unknown Fact:

When Hugh Hefner died, no one said "He's in a better place now..."

□

Unknown Fact:

The best way to save a ton of money on child support is to use condoms.

●

Unknown Fact:

The "Shin bone" was given to us by God to help us find furniture in a dark room.

☒

Unknown Fact:

A "Plick" ...is a guy who doesn't tip in a Chinese restaurant.

□

Unknown Fact:

The quickest way to double your money is to fold it in half.

■

Unknown Fact:

You can save a bunch of money on car insurance, by not buying any.

☒

Unknown Fact:

A Gold digger is like a hooker... only a lot smarter.

●

Unknown Fact:

Lawyers don't really care if you compliment them on their briefcase.

❑

Unknown Fact:

You'll sleep a lot better if you're not awake.

●

Unknown Fact:

Most people would love mornings better if they started later.

〰

Unknown Fact:

People who have more birthdays live longer.

❑

Unknown Fact:

In life, sometimes you're the dog and sometimes you're the hydrant.

■

Unknown Fact:

Nothing in life is friendlier than a WET dog.

Unknown Fact:

When you get a bladder infection, urine trouble.

≋

Unknown Fact:

Most people in the south involved in Incest are "relatively" happy.

❑

Unknown Fact:

A ZEBRA... is the largest size a woman can buy.

Unknown Fact:

Thomas Edison invented the lightbulb 20 years before he got credit for it because he forgot to plug it in.

●

Unknown Fact:

Golf...is nothing but Pool played outdoors.

☐

Unknown Fact:

Two is company, three's The Musketeers.

☒

Unknown Fact:

You have a drinking problem if your idea of Frozen Food is Scotch on the Rocks.

●

Unknown Fact:

A lot of married men get a mistress just to break up the monogamy.

☐

Unknown Fact:

People who live in stone houses shouldn't throw glasses.

Unknown Fact:

Some men like to go fishing but most men like to do their drinking at home.

~

Unknown Fact:

You win some and you lose some, but most prefer getting some.

⊠

Unknown Fact:

Pushing the elevator button more than once does not make it arrive faster.

■

Unknown Fact:

Some kids are good when you give them money and some kids are good for nothing.

~

Unknown Fact:

Christmas is a time when neither the past nor the future is as important as the "Present".

◻

Unknown Fact:

If you give someone who is "kinky" enough rope, they'll tie you up.

○

Unknown Fact:

The only time you have too much fuel is when you're on fire.

■

Unknown Fact:

You can make both Ends Meet but you can't make them Like each other.

●

Unknown Fact:

Sometimes all the early bird gets is up.

❑

Unknown Fact:

A kiss is the shortest distance between two people.

❑

Unknown Fact:

Captain Kirk of Star Trek once shit on the ceiling...because he wanted to "Go" where no man had gone before.

○

Unknown Fact:

A fool and his money can throw a hell of a party.

○

Unknown Fact:

The trouble with being early is nobody's there to appreciate it.

☒

Unknown Fact:

Lawyers believe that a man is innocent until proven broke.

☐

Unknown Fact:

Cell phones ruined the fun of pushing a fully clothed person into a pool.

〰

Unknown Fact:

There's an island in the Pacific where there are no taxes, no unemployment, no crime, no fast food and no hospitals. There's also no inhabitants.

○

Unknown Fact:

There are four ways to become rich: Win the lottery...Inherit it...Earn it....or Sue.

■

Unknown Fact:

Lending money causes amnesia.

■

Unknown Fact:

Today, when kids play Doctor...one operates and the other sues.

□

Unknown Fact:

The worst pickup line in a bar is..."Hi, my penis would like to buy you a drink."

☒

Unknown Fact:

Money can't buy love...but it can certainly make a person more likeable.

◼

Unknown Fact:

It was Moses who was the first to say..."It's not what you know, but who you know."

〰

Unknown Fact:

You never hear people, "It's only a game" when they're winning.

❑

Unknown Fact:

Having plans always sounds like a good idea until you have to get dressed and leave the house.

❑

Unknown Fact:

The best way to make a dollar go farther is to mail it to a friend in Australia.

■

Unknown Fact:

The Indians were the first to say, "There goes the Neighborhood."

〜〜

Unknown Fact:

The term "Vegetarian" is an old Indian word for "Bad Hunter".

○

Unknown Fact:

No one is purfick.

□

Unknown Fact:

Porcupines have to be very careful when making love.

■

Unknown Fact:

Single women can't fart because they don't get an asshole until they get married.

□

Unknown Fact:

"Payola" started when the first kid gave his teacher an apple.

○

Unknown Fact:

It's impossible to nail JELL-O to a tree.

●

Unknown Fact:

Drinking 8 glasses of beer a day is easier than drinking 8 glasses of water a day.

◻

Unknown Fact:

There is such a thing as a Successful Failure.

〰

Unknown Fact:

Old Age doesn't last that long.

○

Unknown Fact:

If you tell a lie and say it's a lie, it's not really a lie.

———

Unknown Fact:

It is still possible for someone with no talent or experience to become a major celebrity.

□

Made in the USA
Middletown, DE
25 September 2022

10961509R00126